THIS CANDLEWICK BOOK BELONGS TO:

_____

_____

_____

_____

For
Tom Deering
who came with
his teddy bears
M. W.

For Sarah
P. D.

First U.S. paperback edition 1998

The Library of Congress has cataloged the hardcover edition as follows:

Waddell, Martin.
When the teddy bears came / Martin Waddell ;
illustrated by Penny Dale.— 1st U.S. ed.
Summary: When Tom's mother brings home the new baby, so many
teddy bears arrive as gifts that there is no room for Tom, but she assures
him that there will always be a place for him.
ISBN 1-56402-529-2 (hardcover)
[1. Teddy bears—Fiction. 2. Babies—Fiction.
3. Brothers and sisters—Fiction.] I. Dale, Penny, ill. II. Title.
PZ7.W1137Wh   1995
[E]—dc20   94-10580

ISBN 0-7636-0462-3 (paperback)

10 9 8 7 6 5 4 3 2 1

Printed in Hong Kong

This book was typeset in Stempel Schneidler.
The pictures were done in watercolor and pencil crayon.

Candlewick Press
2067 Massachusetts Avenue
Cambridge, Massachusetts 02140

When the Teddy Bears Came

Martin Waddell ◆ illustrated by Penny Dale

CANDLEWICK PRESS
CAMBRIDGE, MASSACHUSETTS

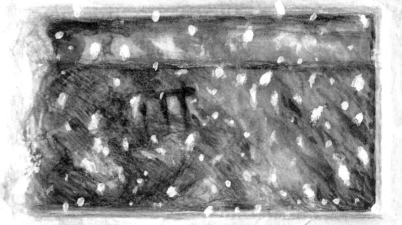

When the new baby came to Tom's house, the teddy bears started coming.

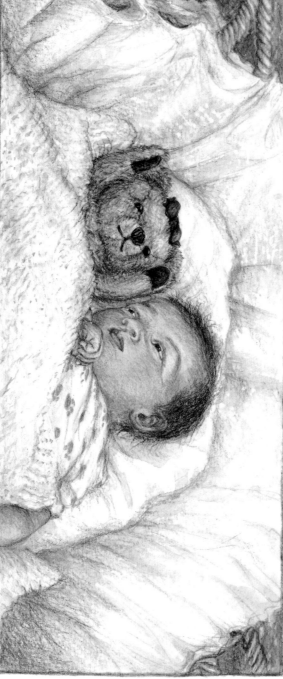

Alice Bear came in the crib.

Tom kissed Alice Bear and the baby.

Ozzie Bear came with Uncle Jack.

Ozzie Bear had a flag and a hat.

Ozzie Bear sat on a chair,

where he could take care of the baby.

Then Miss Wilkins came with Sam Bear in his sailor suit. Sam Bear sat on the chair beside Ozzie Bear.

"I want to give our baby a bear!" Tom said.

So he gave the new baby his Huggy.

Tom told Mom, "Huggy can take care of our baby now."

Tom put Huggy beside Alice Bear.

Rockwell and Dudley Bear came in a van.

They were a little squashed.

Tom unsquashed them for the new baby.

Rockwell and Dudley Bear went on the chair

beside Ozzie Bear and Sam Bear.

Gran brought Bodger Bear from her attic.

"That's my Bodger Bear!" Dad said.

Mom said, "Look at our baby with all of these bears!"

Tom looked at the bears. Alice Bear, Ozzie Bear, Sam Bear and Huggy, Rockwell and Dudley Bear and Dad's Bodger Bear, all on the couch beside Mom and the baby.

"There's no room for *me*," Tom said to Mom.

Mom smiled and said, "Come here, Tom, and sit on my knee. You and I can take care of the bears. It's Dad's turn to take care of the baby."

And that's what they did.
When the new baby
came to Tom's house
they all took turns taking
care of the bears . . .

and together they all looked after the baby.

MARTIN WADDELL wrote *When the Teddy Bears Came* after his sister-in-law brought her new baby home. "Friends dropped by to see the baby, and they all brought bears. As I watched the child become engulfed by bears, the story unfolded before my eyes." Martin Waddell is one of the most popular children's authors of his time, having written more than one hundred books for children, including *Can't You Sleep, Little Bear?; Let's Go Home, Little Bear; Farmer Duck; Owl Babies; The Big Big Sea;* and *Once There Were Giants.*

PENNY DALE always uses real people as models for her illustrations. "For this book," she says, "I had to find a lot of teddy bear models. One was my brother's old bear, one was mine, and so on. Casting them was heartbreaking because I needed only seven and had to tell the others they didn't get the part." She is the author-illustrator of *Daisy Rabbit's Tree House, Ten in the Bed, Ten Out of Bed, All About Alice,* and *Wake Up, Mr. B.!,* as well as the illustrator of *The Mushroom Hunt,* by Simon Frazer, and *Once There Were Giants,* by Martin Waddell.